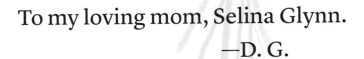

To my loving mom, Selina Glynn.
—D. G.

Library of Congress Cataloging-in-Publication Data available.

ISBN 978-1-4521-7280-4

Manufactured in China.

FSC
www.fsc.org
MIX
Paper from
responsible sources
FSC™ C008047

Design by Jay Marvel.
Typeset in Lyon Text.
The illustrations in this book were rendered in watercolor, cut
paper, pastels, and colored pencils.

10 9 8 7 6 5 4 3 2

Chronicle Books LLC
680 Second Street
San Francisco, California 94107

Chronicle Books—we see things differently.
Become part of our community at www.chroniclekids.com.

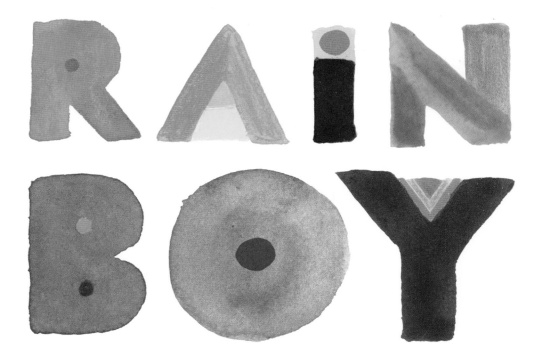

RAIN BOY

Dylan Glynn

chronicle books · san francisco

Once there was a Rain Boy.

Rain Boy was not popular
around the sandbox.

Or the monkey bars. Or the soccer field.

Because of course,
when Rain Boy was
around, it rained.

Sun Kidd
was another story.

Sun Kidd was new.

She was from somewhere on the other side of the planet.

Sun Kidd was the talk of the playground.
She was popular at barbecues, at tea parties,
and at the beach.

Because when Sun was around,
it was sunny.

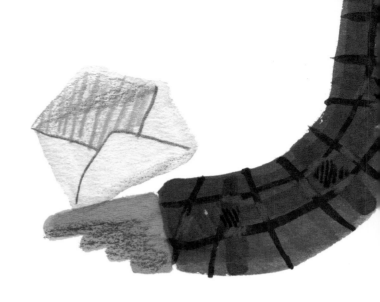

Her birthday was smack-dab in the
middle of summer, and her parents decided to
throw her a big sleepover surprise party.

The whole class was coming!

Rain Boy had never been to a
birthday party before.

And he might never
go to one again.

This wasn't the surprise
anybody had planned.

"Oh no, he's getting everything wet!" cried Olive.
"The cake is melting!" shouted Star.
"The presents are ruined!"

Soon everyone was yelling.

"Rain, Rain, go away!"

Just then, Sun came down
the stairs.

"Cut it out!
Stop yelling at him!"

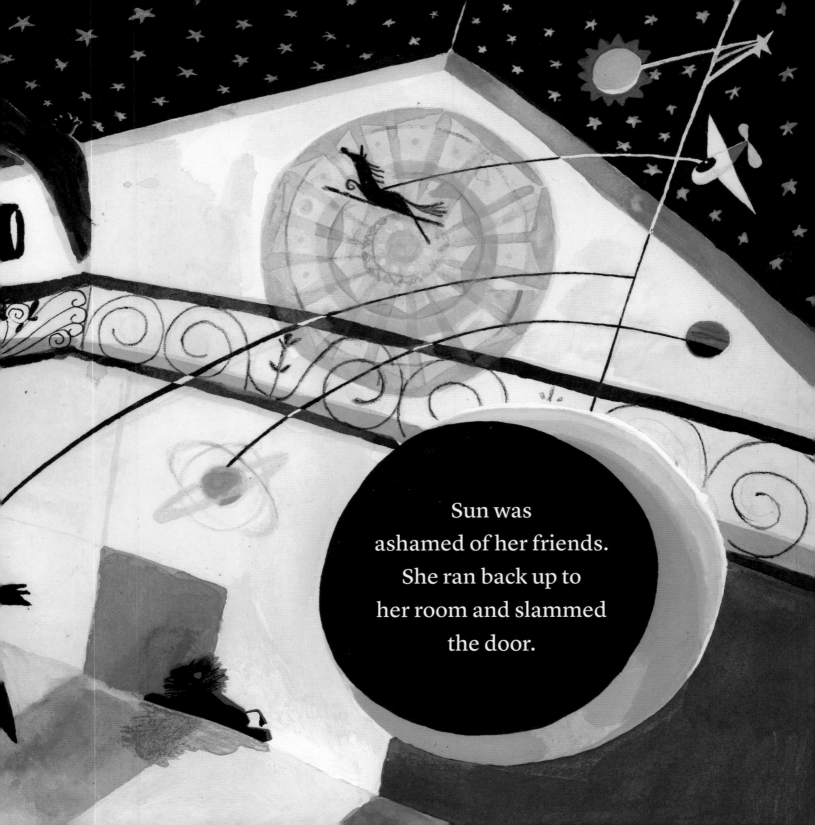

Sun was
ashamed of her friends.
She ran back up to
her room and slammed
the door.

The room
was silent, but
Rain Boy still heard
the words. They looped
over and over in his head.

"Rain, Rain, go away."

And so he did.

A storm began to brew.

Rain Boy didn't come back to school.

Neither did Sun Kidd.

The kids said he must have
kidnapped her.
It didn't matter what Ms. Parks
told them.

A day turned into weeks,
into months of rain. People learned
to live with wetness.

They stayed inside and
drank hot cocoa.

Their flowers bloomed
and their grass turned greener.

They noticed they
were talking to
each other
a lot more.

One by one the neighborhood kids stepped out of their houses and into the streets.

They came out to play in the rain.

In this wet wonderland, flowers and trees were more vibrant.

Beautiful reflections
shimmered and
stretched across streets.
The kids skipped and
stomped through puddles.

One morning, Rain Boy took a deep
breath and peeked outside.
With a big sigh, he stormed a little less hard.

The thunder and lightning stopped.
Only rain now.

Looking at the disheveled town,
Rain Boy felt really tired.

Sun Kidd heard the rain get softer on her roof.
She peeked out of her covers and through the clouds.

"Rain Boy?"

"Look."

It was the first time
Rain Boy felt that people actually
liked having him around.

Rain Boy puffed up with pride.

He decided it was time to be brave.

Play was better together.

So the next time you're feeling down
and your world is dark and gray . . .

just look up.